This book should be returned to any branch of the
Lancashire County Library on or before the date shown

-2 DEC 2014   -2 DEC 2014

2 9 JAN 2015   2 1 MAY 2016   2 9 JUN 2018

2 3 MAR 2015

1 4 AUG 2015

0 3 NOV 2016

2 5 AUG 2015   4 AUG 2018

2 2

10 OCT 20   JG 2018

0 6 DEC 2018

1 3 JAN 20

APR 2018

1 9 MAR 2016   2 3 AUG 2019

2 0 NOV 2019   3 1 OCT 2019

1 1 DEC 2019

LL1(A)

To Sarah B, a true friend

Special thanks to
Rachel Elliot

ORCHARD BOOKS
338 Euston Road, London NW1 3BH
Orchard Books Australia
Level 17/207 Kent Street, Sydney, NSW 2000
A Paperback Original

First published in 2014 by Orchard Books

HiT entertainment

A CIP catalogue record for this book is available
from the British Library.

ISBN 978 1 40833 392 1

1 3 5 7 9 10 8 6 4 2

Printed and bound by CPI Group (UK) Ltd, Croydon, CR0 4YY

MIX
Paper from
responsible sources
FSC® C104740
FSC
www.fsc.org

The paper and board used in this paperback are natural recyclable
products made from wood grown in sustainable forests. The
manufacturing processes conform to the environmental regulations
of the country of origin.

Orchard Books is a division of Hachette Children's Books,
an Hachette UK company

www.hachette.co.uk

Alison
the Art
Fairy

by Daisy Meadows

ORCHARD

www.rainbowmagic.co.uk

The Fairyland Palace

Fairyland School

Tippington Town

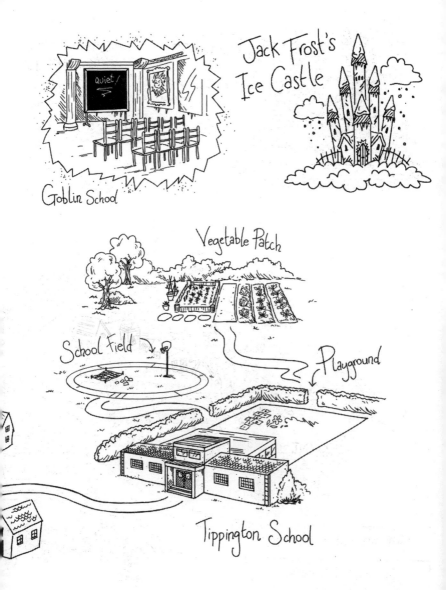

Goblin School

Jack Frost's Ice Castle

Vegetable Patch

School Field

Playground

Tippington School

Jack Frost's Spell

It's time the School Days Fairies see
How wonderful a school should be –
A place where goblins must be bossed,
And learn about the great Jack Frost.

Now every fairy badge of gold
Makes goblins do as they are told.
Let silly fairies whine and wail.
My cleverness will never fail!

Contents

Best Friends Together

"Lunchtime already!" exclaimed Rachel Walker, closing her maths book. "I wonder what sandwiches Mum has packed today."

"I can't believe I'm really here," Kirsty Tate said with a smile, "at school with you!"

Rachel nodded happily. Being in the same class as her best friend really was a dream come true! Kirsty normally went to school in Wetherbury, but heavy rain over the holidays had flooded the classrooms. Now the school was closed for a week while builders repaired the damage and cleaned it up again.

Mrs Tate and Mrs Walker had been chatting on the phone when Rachel came up with the idea of inviting Kirsty to Tippington. By the end of the call it was agreed – Kirsty would stay with the Walkers for the week and go to school there. At first Kirsty had felt a little nervous about starting the term somewhere new, but the thought of sitting next to her best friend in every lesson was so exciting! Since she'd started

yesterday, she'd loved getting to know
Rachel's school. Everybody had been
really friendly, apart from the pair of
naughty goblins that had joined the class
pretending to be new boys! Only Kirsty
and Rachel had worked out who the
screeching voices, pointy noses and green
uniforms really belonged to.

"Get out of my
way!" yelled one
of them now,
barging to the
front of the
class.

"Shan't!"
grunted the
other. "I'm
getting my
lunch first!"

11

Kirsty's teacher, Mr Beaker, frowned at the noisy pair.

"Take turns please," he said sternly. "You'll cause an accident if you push and shove."

The goblins were squabbling so loudly they didn't hear a word that Mr Beaker said. As they struggled to get through the door, they bumped into a table, knocking over a stack of cardboard boxes. Egg cartons, cereal packets and empty tissue boxes tumbled all over the floor. Kirsty and Rachel rushed to pick them back up again.

"Trust the goblins," whispered Rachel. "I hope they don't cause any more trouble."

Kirsty watched the pair barge out of the room with Mr Beaker following after.

"I have a horrible feeling they might," she said ruefully.

During one of their first lessons together, the girls had met someone amazing – Marissa the Science Fairy. Kirsty and Rachel had been friends with

13

the fairies ever since their first holiday
on Rainspell Island. The girls were
always ready to help them outwit Jack
Frost and his army of goblin servants.
This time however, Jack Frost really had
gone a step too far. He'd sent his goblins
to steal four magical gold star badges
belonging to the School Days Fairies
– Marissa and her friends Alison the
Art Fairy, Lydia the Reading Fairy
and Kathryn the PE Fairy. He had a
rotten plan in mind for the badges, too.
The vain Ice Lord had set up his own
school for goblins, filled with lessons all
about him!

The poor School Days Fairies had
been dismayed. They needed their
badges to make subjects interesting and
help lessons to run smoothly. Until the

precious objects were back where they belonged, classes in Fairyland and the human world were in trouble.

"I don't want another science lesson like yesterday," said Rachel, giving a little shudder. The morning had been full of mishaps, until Kirsty and Rachel had worked out what was happening. The rowdy new boys had turned out to be two of Jack's Frost's naughtiest pupils, a pair so full of mischief they'd even been expelled from his goblin school! Before leaving Jack Frost's frozen kingdom, the goblins had pocketed all four magical badges and fled to the human world. Kirsty and Rachel had managed to return one badge to Marissa, but they still needed to find the other three.

"We've got to be ready for anything,"

said Kirsty, picking up an armful of
cardboard. "If the goblins are still
in school, the badges must be here
somewhere, too."

"But Marissa said that King Oberon
and Queen Titania will be visiting
the Fairyland School in a few days,"
remarked Rachel with a sigh. "We have
to get the badges back before then."

"There isn't much time," agreed
Kirsty.

"Time for what?"

The friends spun round. Mr Beaker
had walked back into the classroom!
Rachel's cheeks turned pink. She hoped
that the teacher hadn't overheard their
conversation – nobody else knew about
the fairies. Before she could think of an
answer, Kirsty piped up:

"I was just telling Rachel that it's
time to go out to the
playground!"

Mr Beaker
nodded, then
sat down at his
desk.

"Thanks for
picking up those
boxes, girls,"
he said gratefully.

"I've been collecting them all holiday."

"What are they for?" Rachel wondered aloud.

Now Mr Beaker was the one looking mysterious.

"It's for a special art project," was all he would say. "You'll find out more after lunch."

Kirsty and Rachel exchanged excited smiles. Art was one of their favourite subjects!

As soon as they'd eaten their sandwiches and fruit, Rachel took Kirsty out to the playground.

"Look, there are Amina and Adam!" cried Rachel, pointing to her friends.

"Shall we go and say hello?" suggested Kirsty.

Amina and Adam were in a quiet

corner, kneeling side-by-side on the tarmac.

"Mr Beaker said we could use our chalks to create some playground art," explained Amina, "as long as we wash it off every Friday."

"Or it rains first!" grinned Adam, pointing up to the sky.

Amina handed a packet of chalk to Rachel and Kirsty. "Fancy a go?"

The girls both replied at once. "Yes, please!"

"I know just what to draw," declared Rachel, pulling out a red chalk. "A fairy!"

She imagined Ruby the Red Fairy

fluttering in the sky.
She could just
picture the
shape of
her dainty
wings and
the rosebuds
in her hair.
Beside her,
Kirsty tipped out
the rest of the colours.

"Why don't I draw a rainbow for the fairy to fly over?" she said.

Rachel beamed. She couldn't help but notice the secret twinkle in Kirsty's eye! Soon, the girls' chalk picture began to take shape.

"Something's not right," said Rachel, standing back to look at it properly.

Somehow Ruby's cheerful face had creased up into a frown! Her wand was crooked, too.

"My poor rainbow," sighed Kirsty, "it's turned into a smudgy mess!"

Amina and Adam weren't doing much better. They had tried to chalk a happy farmyard scene, but it had just come out as a scribble.

"I don't want to do this any more," said Adam, putting down the chalks and running off. "Let's go and play on

the climbing frame."

Amina followed him, leaving Rachel
and Kirsty to themselves.

Rachel wrinkled her nose. "I would
never draw Ruby without a smile,"
she remarked. "Do you think this
has something to do with the missing
badges?"

"Y-yes!" stuttered Kirsty, grasping
Rachel's arm and pointing down to her
chalk rainbow.

Rachel gasped. The blurry pinks,
yellows and blues had started to shimmer
and glow! A magical haze billowed
over the ground, glinting with colourful
twinkles. A tiny dot in the middle started
to get bigger and bigger until…*ting!* A
magical fairy appeared!

Puzzling Pictures

As soon as she spotted Kirsty and Rachel, the fairy did a happy twirl.

"Hello again!" she chimed in a singsong voice. "I'm so pleased I found you!"

The fairy waved her wand with a flourish. A cloud of tiny artist's palettes instantly popped into the air around her. Each one was a perfect miniature, complete with brushes and ovals of brightly coloured paint.

"We met yesterday, didn't we?" said Kirsty, remembering their trip to the Fairyland School.

"You're Alison," added Rachel, "Alison the Art Fairy!"

Alison giggled with pleasure. She really did look as pretty as a picture. Her sunny blonde hair tumbled in waves around her shoulders, topped off with a dusty pink beret. She wore a bright dotty T-shirt with a slogan on it, jangly beads and a maxi skirt in different shades of blue.

"It's tie-dye," she said proudly, when she noticed Kirsty and Rachel admiring her skirt. "I made it myself!"

The cheerful little fairy was full of chatter, until the messy chalk drawings on the ground caught her eye.

"Oh dear," she said forlornly. "You can probably guess why I'm here."

Kirsty glanced nervously over her shoulder, then knelt down next to Alison.

"Is it your gold star badge?"

Alison nodded furiously.

"I really must get it back. My magical badge makes sure that all art lessons are full of fun and go smoothly! Imagine a world without lovely pictures, sculptures and models. What a dreadful, dreary thought…"

With that, the fairy's voice trailed off into silence. Rachel glimpsed the tiniest silver tear trickle down Alison's cheek.

"We'll put things right," she replied kindly. "The goblins can't get away with this!"

Kirsty took Rachel's hand, her face full of determination.

"We'll find your badge in no time," she promised.

Alison's face brightened at once. Before she could say another word, however, a group of children ran past.

28

"You need to hide," whispered Rachel.
"Can you fly into my
pocket?"

Quick as a flash,
Alison darted
into Rachel's
blazer pocket
and ducked out
of sight. A trail of
tiny stars glittered
in the air behind
her for just a second,
disappearing one by one.

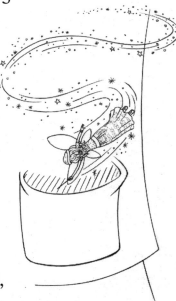

Kirsty and Rachel waited as more of
their schoolmates galloped past them. A
big circle of children had formed on the
other side of the playground. Even Adam
and Amina had jumped down from the
climbing frame to go and join the crowd.

"What's happening over there?" asked
Rachel, catching Amina's arm.

"It's the new boys," she answered
breathlessly. "Come and see what
they've done!"

"Is it something naughty?" guessed
Kirsty.

"Oh no," replied Adam. "They've
made the most amazing chalk drawing
ever!"

Kirsty raised an eyebrow at Rachel.

"The goblins are up to something already," she said just loudly enough for Alison to hear.

Kirsty and Rachel grabbed their rucksacks and ran over to get a better look.

"What do you think?" squawked one of the goblins, spotting their curious faces. "Bit better than your silly scribbles!"

"Who'd want to draw a soppy fairy anyway?" barked the other one. "Our drawings are the best!"

For once, the goblins were absolutely right. The tarmac was covered with the most eye-catching, astonishing chalk art they had ever seen.

"It's Jack Frost's Ice Castle," gasped Rachel.

Every detail was perfect. The castle had spiky turrets, frosty icicles and a forbidding oak door. The picture glistened in blues, whites and silvers, creating a feel so wintry it made Kirsty shiver.

"Look," she whispered under her breath, "they've even added the new goblin school. There's the play area at the side."

"No goblin could have drawn this on his own," added Rachel.

"They must have Alison's gold star badge on them right now!" Kirsty replied urgently.

Kirsty gazed at the two smug goblins, preening over their handiwork. Although the other children didn't recognise the Ice Castle, they couldn't help but be impressed by the glittering colours and intricate shapes. Kirsty edged a little closer to the bigger and more boastful goblin.

"I'll sign autographs if you want," he was crowing to the crowd, "but only if you give me some sweets!"

Kirsty blinked. She was sure she could glimpse the tip of the magical badge poking out of his green trouser pocket!

"I think I can get it," she mouthed to Rachel, reaching out her hand.

Kirsty's fingers trembled as she got closer and closer to the badge. Rachel held her breath...

A Sticky Situation

Rrrinnnggg!

Quick as a flash, Kirsty pulled back her hand. The goblin with the magical badge groaned as the children picked up their rucksacks and drifted away.

"Don't go!" he yelled. "Watch me draw something else. Look at how brilliant I am!"

"That's the bell for the end of lunch," said Rachel firmly. "We've got to go back to class."

The goblin blew a raspberry at her and followed his friend inside. The naughty pair didn't even bother to pick up their chalks before they left.

"I was so close," sighed Kirsty, when she and Rachel got back to the cloakroom. Alison peeped out of her hiding place.

"It was a very good try," she said cheerfully. "If that bell had rung a second later, you would have definitely got my badge back."

Rachel gave Kirsty's hand an encouraging squeeze. "At least we know where the badge is now," she said. "We've just got to outsmart those goblins."

Alison pointed her wand towards the school building. "Time to hide again," she reminded them. "Mr Beaker is starting the lesson."

When Kirsty and Rachel walked back into the classroom, there was an excited buzz in the air. Mr Beaker had covered the tables with old newspapers and laid out glue pots, scissors and paintbrushes. In the middle of every table he'd also stacked up interesting piles of old boxes, cardboard tubes and empty food packets.

The children laughed and chatted as they put on their art aprons. Some

picked up the boxes on their table and
started to play with them. Across the
room, the silly goblins were using an old
kitchen roll tube as a pretend sword, then
bashing each other over the head.

"They're making mischief already,"
warned Kirsty. "Look."

Mr Beaker clapped his hands three
times, then waited for everybody to settle
down.

"This afternoon I'm setting you an art challenge," he announced. "Every table should work together as a group. You have one hour to use the cardboard boxes in the middle to make a model vehicle. The group who makes the best one will get a gold star and the vehicle will be put on display for the school inspector's visit in two days' time."

The teacher held up a model of a car that he'd made earlier.

"I stuck this together myself, then painted the outside with blue paint," he continued. "I bet you can come up with something even more creative...oh!"

Before Mr Beaker could finish talking, the car's wheels dropped off! One by one, all four of the disks went tumbling across the classroom.

"I don't know what happened there," he muttered, sitting down to get a better look at the little car. At the same moment, the pile of spare boxes on the desk beside him fell over. Mr Beaker winced as an empty egg box bounced off his head. *Bop!*

The goblins roared with laughter. Their hoots got even louder when the egg box landed on top of Mr Beaker's junk model car, breaking it into bits.

"How strange," the teacher mumbled

to himself, looking sad. "I'm sure it was stuck tight…"

"Are you all right, Mr Beaker?" asked Rachel.

"Yes, thank you," he replied. "OK class, time to get started."

Kirsty and Rachel were in a group with Adam and Amina. They passed around the boxes on their table, wondering what to make.

"Why don't we forget about wheels," suggested Kirsty, "and make a sailboat instead? We always see lovely ones when we go on holiday. Do you remember, Rachel?"

Rachel's face lit up. She'd never forget the pretty sailboats on Rainspell Island!

"Oh, yes!" she exclaimed. "We could use this shoebox as the boat, then cut the sails out of cereal packets."

"I'll trim out the sails," offered Adam.

"Shall I start on the boat?" replied
Amina, reaching for the shoebox. She
leant over to take the box from Rachel,
when an ugly green hand grabbed the
other side.

"I want that!" snapped a goblin voice.
"We need it for our rocket!"

Before Rachel and Amina could argue, the goblin had stuffed the shoebox under his arm and scuttled back to his table.

"Let him have it," said Kirsty. "We can use this porridge carton instead."

She reached for the glue pot, but somehow it tipped over, covering the table and boxes in white goo.

"It's gone everywhere!" exclaimed
Rachel.

The group tried to peel the glue off,
but lots of the boxes tore and broke into
sticky pieces.

"What a terrible start," groaned
Amina.

"Look at my sails," added Adam.
"They're all stuck together in a big
wedge."

Rachel and Kirsty felt their hearts thump. This art class was a disaster!

Model
Magic

While Adam and Amina tried to rescue the sailboat, Rachel and Kirsty moved their chairs closer together.

"We're not the only ones having trouble," Kirsty whispered into her best friend's ear. "Look over there."

Rachel turned to the next table. Dylan, Maya and Zac were trying to build a junk model train, but they couldn't get the carriages to stick together.

"What's wrong with this glue?" frowned Maya. "It makes my fingers sticky, but it won't work on the cardboard!"

"We have to get Alison's magical star badge back," said Rachel.

"And three guesses where to start searching…" replied Kirsty, pointing to the goblins' table.

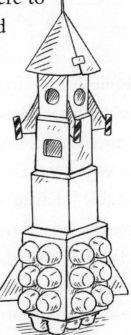

The naughty new boys were working on the tallest junk model rocket the girls had ever seen. The body was made of several boxes glued together, then painted white.

There was a rolled-up piece of card at the top for a nose cone and a row of eggbox engines around the bottom. There were even windows and a door hatch cut out of the sides. As the smug goblins added the last finishing touches, they kept stopping to jeer and boo at everybody else's mishaps.

Rachel peeped across at the biggest goblin. Alison's magical star badge must still be in his trouser pocket! Nothing else would explain his amazing art project.

"I'm going to wash my paintbrush," she said quietly. "That way I'll be able to get a closer look at them."

Rachel pushed her
chair back just
as Mr Beaker
was walking
past with a
pot of green
paint. *Splat!*
Rachel's
elbow knocked
his arm,
sending the pot spinning across the floor.

"Careful!" he cried.

Tears sprung in Rachel's eyes. "Oh
gosh!" she sobbed. "Mr Beaker, I am so
sorry!"

Mr Beaker steadied himself, then
stepped out of the paint puddle.

"It's OK," he smiled. "It was an
accident. Adam and Amina, would you

run to the caretaker's office and fetch me a mop and bucket?"

"I'll get some paper towels," said Kirsty.

The girls tried their best to mop up the paint with the towels, but there was too much of it. As Kirsty stepped back to avoid the green puddle, she skidded on the slippery floor.

"Watch out!" she shouted, sliding right across the room. Kirsty put out her hands to stop herself, but it was too late.

Her arm caught the goblins' rocket, knocking it off the table!

"Oi!" screeched the biggest goblin, stepping forward to catch the model just in the nick of time. He instantly turned round to his goblin friend and jabbed him in the tummy. "That was all your fault!"

The other goblin was furious. "No it wasn't!" he shouted back.

Kirsty breathed a sigh of relief. The silly pair hadn't realised that *she* had knocked it!

"Over here!" she whispered to Rachel, ducking behind the boxes on Mr Beaker's desk.

Rachel rushed over. As soon as the friends were hidden out of sight, Alison flitted out of Rachel's blazer pocket.

"Stay still," she said urgently. "I'm going to turn you into fairies."

Rachel and Kirsty held hands. Suddenly a fountain of fairydust fizzed all around them, covering them in a sparkling shower of pink and gold.

"It's happening," murmured Rachel. "We're getting smaller!"

Blast Off!

In the blink of an eye, Kirsty and Rachel had shrunk down to fairy size. Kirsty unfurled her delicate wings and smiled. It felt wonderful to be magical again!

"Thank you," gushed Rachel, fluttering over to give Alison a hug.

Alison giggled with pleasure.

"If we're all tiny," she reasoned, "Mr Beaker won't notice if you take some time out to try and save his art class."

"Let's get closer to those goblins," suggested Kirsty, taking Rachel and Alison's hands.

The fairies flitted across the classroom as fast as their wings would take them. One by one, they darted into the door hatch cut into the side of the goblins' model rocket. There was just enough room for them to fly up into the centre and peep out of the cardboard windows.

Rachel hoped that the goblins wouldn't see the three little clouds of fairy dust hanging in the air, but she needn't have worried. The cranky new boys were still so busy arguing, they didn't spot a thing!

"I wonder where my badge is?" asked Alison, popping her little head out of the rocket window.

"It can't be far away," answered Rachel.

Suddenly Kirsty had a clever idea. She fluttered up inside the nose cone and, using all her might, pushed the rolled-up card off the top of the rocket.

"Perhaps if the rocket needs fixing, the goblins will *have* to use the magical gold star badge!" she declared.

"Good thinking," agreed Rachel, flying down to the bottom of the rocket. With a giant fairy heave, she managed to push the eggbox engines away from the base.

At that very moment, a deafening shout shook the model from top to bottom.

"What's happened here?" roared the bigger goblin, noticing the damage. "Who's been spoiling my rocket?"

"Don't start blaming me again," complained his friend.

As the big goblin picked the rocket up to take a closer look, the loose eggbox engines dropped off the bottom. His face turned a horrible purple colour.

"It *is* you!" he fumed, pushing the other goblin back on his chair.

The small goblin was indignant. "Why would I want to do that?" he argued, before grumbling under his breath, "Probably knocked it off with your own clumsy mitts."

Kirsty, Rachel and Alison clung onto the cardboard walls inside the rocket, their hearts pounding.

"It's obviously not me!" barked the big goblin. "How could I mess up the rocket when I've got the fairies' magical star badge?"

With that, the goblin pulled Alison's badge out of his trouser pocket and waved it in the air.

"This could be our chance," gasped Alison, pointing out of the rocket window.

But suddenly, they found themselves on the move again. Grabbing the broken pieces and a glue pot in one hand, and the rocket with the fairies inside in the other, the goblin raced across the classroom. He tore straight past Amina and Adam with the mop and bucket, right out of the school building.

"What is he doing now?" cried
Kirsty. "Pupils can't leave class without
permission!"

The friends were rocked about terribly
as the goblin ran faster and faster. He
headed into the playground, before
finally setting the rocket down next
to the climbing frame. As soon as the
model was steady, Alison, Kirsty and
Rachel snuck out of the hatch door and
flitted out of sight. With a wave of her
wand, Alison turned the girls back to
human size.

Kirsty and Rachel ducked behind the
climbing frame and waited. Thinking he
was alone, the goblin crouched on the
ground and started to glue the broken
pieces of cardboard back into place.

"This rocket was all my idea," he muttered. "Wait 'til they see it fly through the sky!"

As soon as he'd put the model back together again, the goblin started to clamber up the climbing frame. Rachel spotted her chance.

"Hey!" she called. "What are you doing with that amazing rocket?"

The goblin's face broke into a proud smirk.

"Bet you wish you'd made it!" he taunted. "Look at all the awesome features I've added."

Rachel winked at Kirsty. Goblins really were the vainest creatures in the world! The new boy couldn't resist showing off every detail of his model. While he droned on about how clever he was, Alison fluttered up behind him.

"I think I can get it," she mouthed silently, pointing to the badge sticking out of the goblin's pocket.

The goblin's face suddenly filled with mischief. Before Alison could swoop down and take it, he rummaged in his pocket, pulled out the badge and held it up in the air!

Enchanted Skies

"Know what this is?" bragged the goblin, waving the Art Fairy's gold star badge under Rachel and Kirsty's noses.

Both girls nervously shook their heads. Poor Alison fluttered silently around the back of the goblin, then hid herself in the bib of Kirsty's apron.

"It's a badge, you dopes!" continued the new boy. "With this, I can make my rocket fly. And not just some silly distance, either. This will make it soar right across the playground!"

Rachel summoned up all her courage. She stepped closer, trying to look unimpressed by the goblin's claims.

"If the badge is *really* magic," she challenged, "surely it's got to be inside the rocket somewhere to make it fly?"

Irritated, the goblin thought for a minute. Rachel was right! Then he remembered his clever door hatch.

"Watch this!" he crowed, opening the little door and shoving the magical badge inside. The goblin lifted the rocket high in the air and hurled it up as far as he could.

"Well done, Rachel!" chimed a silvery voice.

Alison burst out from Kirsty's apron and darted into the air. She waved her wand in a circle, sending starbursts and twinkly paint palettes fizzing in all directions.

"Look at the rocket now," gasped Rachel, pointing up to the sky.

Alison's magic had sent the model flying in a loop the loop, just like the movement of her wand.

"Are you ready, Kirsty?" she asked, her eyes dancing with excitement.

"Stop it!" barked the goblin.

The rocket arched over the play area before gliding gently down into Kirsty's outstretched hands. Kirsty immediately opened the door hatch and pulled out the magical badge.

"Here you are, Alison," she giggled.

Alison bobbed politely and touched the badge with her wand. It shrank down to fairy size at once. The

delighted fairy fluttered and somersaulted
above the girls' heads, filling the air with
joyful sparkles of colour.

The goblin swiped
feebly at the fairy,
but he knew the
game was up.

"Trust you two to
ruin everything," he
shouted, sticking his
tongue out at Kirsty
and Rachel.

"At least you've got your
rocket," said Kirsty, handing
the model back to the disgruntled goblin.

"We need to go back inside, Alison,"
called Rachel. "See you soon!"

"Good riddance!" blurted out the
goblin.

Alison blew the girls a kiss and disappeared into the afternoon sky. Kirsty and Rachel skipped back into class, but the goblin didn't follow them. Instead, he got back to launching his precious toy. He threw the rocket up into the air, but without any fairy magic it crashed straight back down to the ground again.

By the end of the afternoon, Mr Beaker's classroom was a much nicer place to be. Apart from the grumpy goblin in the corner, everybody was working quietly and happily on their model vehicles.

"He's still out there," whispered Rachel, pointing out of the classroom window. The big goblin was still storming up and down the playground with his rocket.

"Some goblins never learn," chuckled Kirsty, fitting the mast onto their model boat. She beamed across at Adam and Amina. Their vehicle had beautiful rainbow sails, a cabin in the middle and a row of round portholes.

Mr Beaker stood up in front of the whiteboard.

"And the winner for best art project is…Dylan, Maya and Zac's terrific passenger train!"

Kirsty and Rachel clapped enthusiastically. The train really did look sensational!

71

"The vehicle will be displayed in pride of place in the school foyer," added Mr Beaker, "in time for the school inspector's visit."

"But we're not ready for the inspector yet!" whispered Rachel. "The School Days Fairies are still missing two badges!"

Kirsty held out her little finger, linking it up with her best friend's. It was the girls' way of making very special promises to each other.

"We'll find those magical badges before I go home," she declared. "You and I will never give up on the fairies!"

Now it's time for Kirsty and Rachel to help...

Lydia the Reading Fairy

Read on for a sneak peek...

"I love the smell of libraries, don't you?" said Kirsty Tate.

She took a deep breath and looked around at the bookshelves of the Tippington School library. Her best friend, Rachel Walker, smiled at her.

"I love having you here at school with me," she said. "I wish it was for longer than a week!"

It was only the third day of the new term, and it had already turned into the most fun and exciting term Rachel had ever known. She had lots of friends at Tippington School, but none of them was as special as Kirsty. She had often wished that they could go to the same school. Then Kirsty's school had been flooded, and the builders had said that the repairs were going to take a week. So for five happy days the best friends were at school together at last.

Read **Lydia the Reading Fairy** to find out what adventures are in store for Kirsty and Rachel!

RAINBOW *magic*

Join in the magic online by signing up to the Rainbow Magic fan club!

Sign up today at:
www.rainbowmagicbooks.co.uk

Meet the
School Days Fairies

Kirsty and Rachel are going to school together! Can they get back the School Days Fairies' magical objects from Jack Frost, and keep lessons fun for everyone?

www.rainbowmagicbooks.co.uk

Competition!

The School Days Fairies have created a special
competition just for you!

Collect all four books in the School Days Fairies series
and answer the special questions in the back of each one.

Once you have all the answers, take the first letter from
each one and arrange them to spell a secret word!
When you have the answer, go online and enter!

Where did Kirsty and Rachel first meet the fairies?

_ _ _ _ _ _ _

_ _ _ _ _ _

We will put all the correct entries into a draw and select
a winner to receive a special Rainbow Magic Goody Bag
featuring lots of treats for you and your fairy friends.
You'll also feature in a new Rainbow Magic story!

Enter online now at www.rainbowmagicbooks.co.uk

Have you read them all?

The Rainbow Fairies
1. Ruby the Red Fairy ☐
2. Amber the Orange Fairy ☐
3. Saffron the Yellow Fairy ☐
4. Fern the Green Fairy ☐
5. Sky the Blue Fairy ☐
6. Izzy the Indigo Fairy ☐
7. Heather the Violet Fairy ☐

The Weather Fairies
8. Crystal the Snow Fairy ☐
9. Abigail the Breeze Fairy ☐
10. Pearl the Cloud Fairy ☐
11. Goldie the Sunshine Fairy ☐
12. Evie the Mist Fairy ☐
13. Storm the Lightning Fairy ☐
14. Hayley the Rain Fairy ☐

The Party Fairies
15. Cherry the Cake Fairy ☐
16. Melodie the Music Fairy ☐
17. Grace the Glitter Fairy ☐
18. Honey the Sweet Fairy ☐
19. Polly the Party Fun Fairy ☐
20. Phoebe the Fashion Fairy ☐
21. Jasmine the Present Fairy ☐

The Jewel Fairies
22. India the Moonstone Fairy ☐
23. Scarlett the Garnet Fairy ☐
24. Emily the Emerald Fairy ☐
25. Chloe the Topaz Fairy ☐
26. Amy the Amethyst Fairy ☐
27. Sophie the Sapphire Fairy ☐
28. Lucy the Diamond Fairy ☐

The Pet Keeper Fairies
29. Katie the Kitten Fairy ☐
30. Bella the Bunny Fairy ☐
31. Georgia the Guinea Pig Fairy ☐
32. Lauren the Puppy Fairy ☐
33. Harriet the Hamster Fairy ☐
34. Molly the Goldfish Fairy ☐
35. Penny the Pony Fairy ☐

The Fun Day Fairies
36. Megan the Monday Fairy
37. Tallulah the Tuesday Fairy
38. Willow the Wednesday Fairy
39. Thea the Thursday Fairy
40. Freya the Friday Fairy
41. Sienna the Saturday Fairy
42. Sarah the Sunday Fairy

The Petal Fairies
43. Tia the Tulip Fairy
44. Pippa the Poppy Fairy
45. Louise the Lily Fairy
46. Charlotte the Sunflower Fairy
47. Olivia the Orchid Fairy
48. Danielle the Daisy Fairy
49. Ella the Rose Fairy

The Dance Fairies
50. Bethany the Ballet Fairy
51. Jade the Disco Fairy
52. Rebecca the Rock'n'Roll Fairy
53. Tasha the Tap Dance Fairy
54. Jessica the Jazz Fairy
55. Saskia the Salsa Fairy
56. Imogen the Ice Dance Fairy

The Sporty Fairies
57. Helena the Horseriding Fairy
58. Francesca the Football Fairy
59. Zoe the Skating Fairy
60. Naomi the Netball Fairy
61. Samantha the Swimming Fairy
62. Alice the Tennis Fairy
63. Gemma the Gymnastics Fairy

The Music Fairies
64. Poppy the Piano Fairy
65. Ellie the Guitar Fairy
66. Fiona the Flute Fairy
67. Danni the Drum Fairy
68. Maya the Harp Fairy
69. Victoria the Violin Fairy
70. Sadie the Saxophone Fairy

The Magical Animal Fairies

71. Ashley the Dragon Fairy ☐
72. Lara the Black Cat Fairy ☐
73. Erin the Firebird Fairy ☐
74. Rihanna the Seahorse Fairy ☐
75. Sophia the Snow Swan Fairy ☐
76. Leona the Unicorn Fairy ☐
77. Caitlin the Ice Bear Fairy ☐

The Green Fairies

78. Nicole the Beach Fairy ☐
79. Isabella the Air Fairy ☐
80. Edie the Garden Fairy ☐
81. Coral the Reef Fairy ☐
82. Lily the Rainforest Fairy ☐
83. Carrie the Snow Cap Fairy ☐
84. Milly the River Fairy ☐

The Ocean Fairies

85. Ally the Dolphin Fairy ☐
86. Amelie the Seal Fairy ☐
87. Pia the Penguin Fairy ☐
88. Tess the Sea Turtle Fairy ☐
89. Stephanie the Starfish Fairy ☐
90. Whitney the Whale Fairy ☐
91. Courtney the Clownfish Fairy ☐

The Twilight Fairies

92. Ava the Sunset Fairy ☐
93. Lexi the Firefly Fairy ☐
94. Zara the Starlight Fairy ☐
95. Morgan the Midnight Fairy ☐
96. Yasmin the Night Owl Fairy ☐
97. Maisie the Moonbeam Fairy ☐
98. Sabrina the Sweet Dreams Fairy ☐

The Showtime Fairies

99. Madison the Magic Show Fairy ☐
100. Leah the Theatre Fairy ☐
101. Alesha the Acrobat Fairy ☐
102. Darcey the Dance Diva Fairy ☐
103. Taylor the Talent Show Fairy ☐
104. Amelia the Singing Fairy ☐
105. Isla the Ice Star Fairy ☐

The Princess Fairies

106. Honor the Happy Days Fairy ☐
107. Demi the Dressing-Up Fairy ☐
108. Anya the Cuddly Creatures Fairy ☐
109. Elisa the Adventure Fairy ☐
110. Lizzie the Sweet Treats Fairy ☐
111. Maddie the Playtime Fairy ☐
112. Eva the Enchanted Ball Fairy ☐

The Pop Star Fairies

113. Jessie the Lyrics Fairy ☐
114. Adele the Singing Coach Fairy ☐
115. Vanessa the Dance Steps Fairy ☐
116. Miley the Stylist Fairy ☐
117. Frankie the Make-Up Fairy ☐
118. Rochelle the Star Spotter Fairy ☐
119. Una the Concert Fairy ☐

The Fashion Fairies

120. Miranda the Beauty Fairy ☐
121. Claudia the Accessories Fairy ☐
12.2. Tyra the Dress Designer Fairy ☐
123. Alexa the Fashion Reporter Fairy ☐
124. Matilda the Hair Stylist Fairy ☐
125. Brooke the Photographer Fairy ☐
126. Lola the Fashion Fairy ☐

The Sweet Fairies

127. Lottie the Lollipop Fairy ☐
128. Esme the Ice Cream Fairy ☐
129. Coco the Cupcake Fairy ☐
130. Clara the Chocolate Fairy ☐
131. Madeleine the Cookie Fairy ☐
132. Layla the Candyfloss Fairy ☐
133. Nina the Birthday Cake Fairy ☐

The Baby Animal Rescue Fairies

134. Mae the Panda Fairy ☐
135. Kitty the Tiger Fairy ☐
136. Mara the Meerkat Fairy ☐
137. Savannah the Zebra Fairy ☐
138. Kimberley the Koala Fairy ☐
139. Rosie the Honey Bear Fairy ☐
140. Anna the Arctic Fox Fairy ☐

The Magical Crafts Fairies

141. Kayla the Pottery Fairy ☐
142. Annabelle the Drawing Fairy ☐
143. Zadie the Sewing Fairy ☐
144. Josie the Jewellery-Making Fairy ☐
145. Violet the Painting Fairy ☐
146. Libby the Story-Writing Fairy ☐
147. Roxie the Baking Fairy ☐

The School Days Fairies

141. Marissa the Science Fairy ☐
142. Alison the Art Fairy ☐
143. Lydia the Reading Fairy ☐
144. Kathryn the PE Fairy ☐

Giselle the Christmas Ballet Fairy

Meet Giselle the Christmas Ballet Fairy! Can Rachel and Kirsty help get her magical items back from Jack Frost in time for the Fairyland Christmas Eve performance?

www.rainbowmagicbooks.co.uk